STEVE GOES TO CARNIVAL

JOSHUA BUTTON AND ROBYN WELLS

CANDLEWICK PRESS

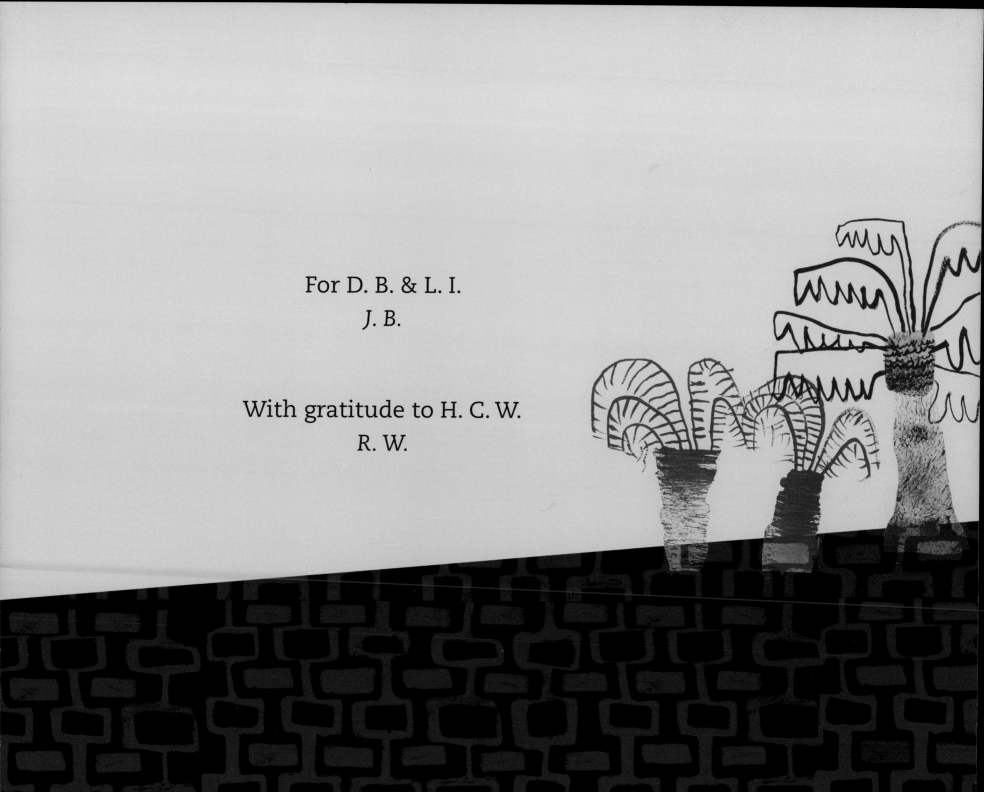

For D. B. & L. I.
J. B.

With gratitude to H. C. W.
R. W.

It is Saturday afternoon at the zoo in Rio.

The jaguars pace in their enclosure.

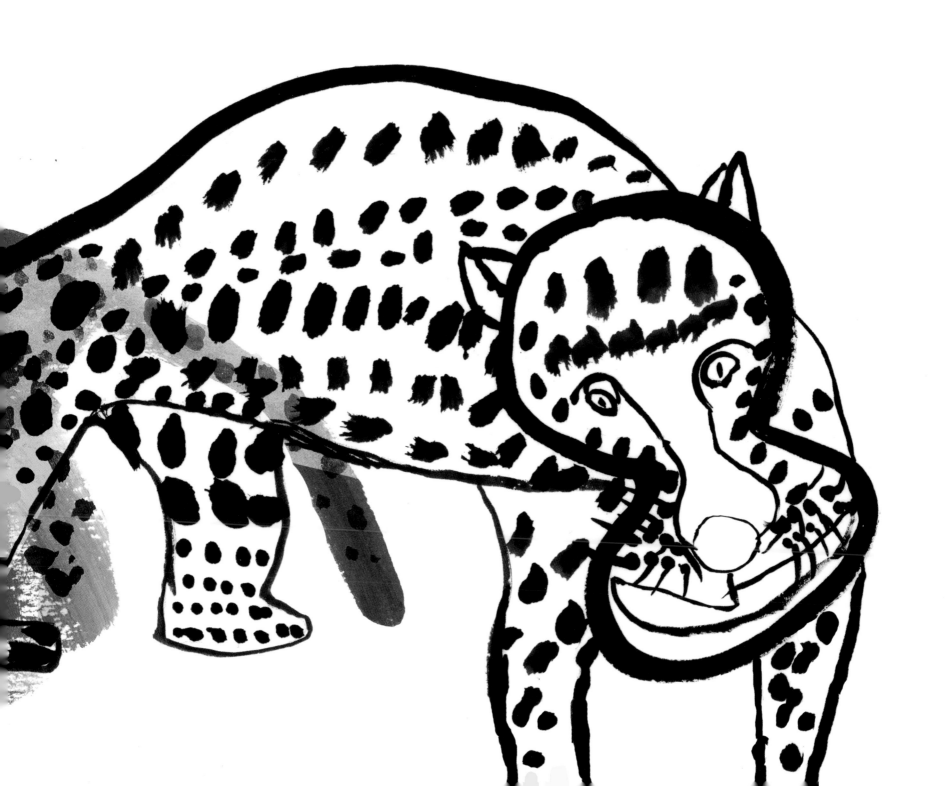

POR FAVOR NÃO ALIMENTE O ELEFANTE

PLEASE DO NOT FEED THE ELEPHANT

The elephant stretches out her trunk for an ice-cream cone.

The howler monkeys hoot and chatter,

and the sloths sway slowly
from side to side.

In the evening, Antonio the zookeeper feeds the animals.

The anteater flicks up ants with his long, sticky tongue.

The elephant trumpets greedily,
and the old lion licks his lips.

Antonio loves all the animals in the zoo, but he loves Steve most of all.

And Steve loves Antonio.

"Hello, my friend!" cries Antonio.

He sets down a bucket of bamboo shoots and his little yellow radio.

Steve switches the radio on and turns up the volume.

Antonio and Steve love all kinds of music, but they love jazz most of all.

They sit back and listen to the sound of a saxophone drifting up into the night sky.

After Antonio has left,
Steve feels the quiet of the night.

He lifts the latch of the cage door,
and out it swings!

Steve clambers up and over the zoo
wall to look for Antonio.

At the tram stop outside the zoo,
Steve finds a wide-brimmed hat.

It is the perfect disguise.

Steve waves down a tram and clambers aboard.

The old yellow tram shudders down the hillside . . .

past the favelas,

and into the city.

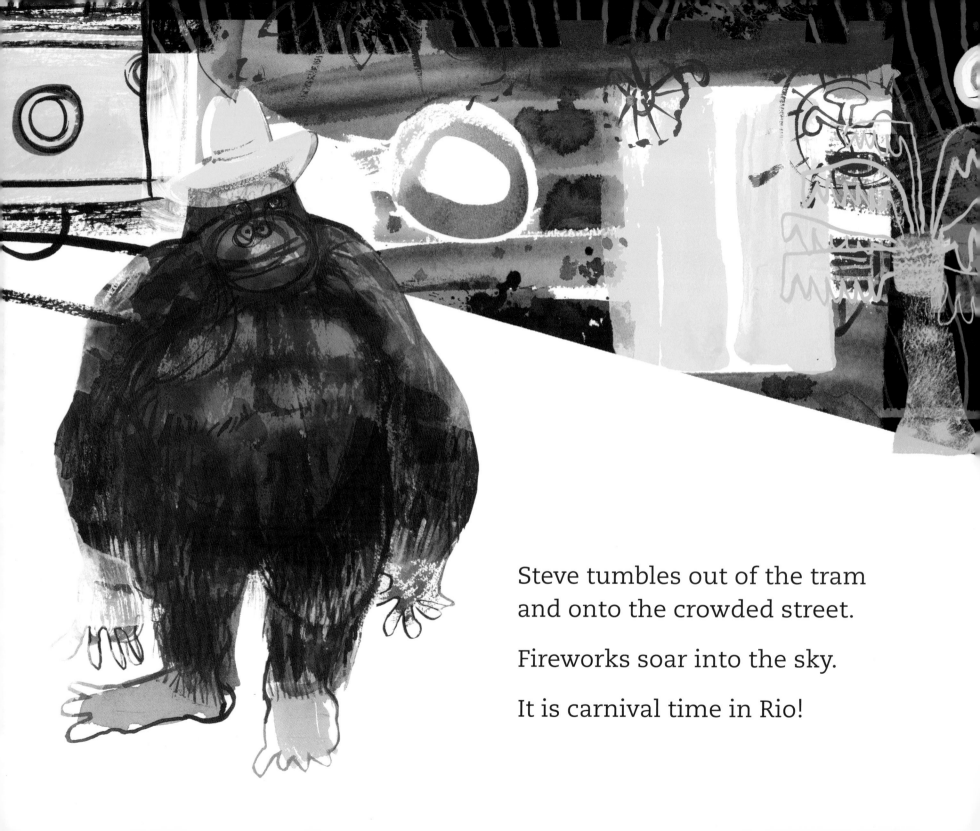

Steve tumbles out of the tram
and onto the crowded street.

Fireworks soar into the sky.

It is carnival time in Rio!

Dancers in sparkling sequins and feather headdresses shimmy along the avenue.

The air shakes with the thud of bass drums,
the rattle of tambourines,
the honk of trombones,
and the shrill of samba whistles.

"Feliz Carnaval!" the sambistas cry out to Steve.

FELIZ CARNAVAL!

"Feliz Carnaval!" cries Steve as he heads off to look for Antonio.

He wends his way through street stalls selling black bean soup . . .

coconut sweets, and chocolate bonbons.

Suddenly Steve stops and listens.

Above the noise of Carnival, he hears the whoop and holler of a saxophone coming from a jazz club across the street.

The doorman at the Blue Jaguar Jazz Club smiles at Steve.

"Entra, senhor!" he says as he waves Steve inside.

Steve pauses to greet the elegant hostess,
and then he hurries across the room.

A jazz quartet is playing.

The piano tinkles,
the double bass pounds,
the saxophone wails,
and the singer hums and trills.

The saxofonista tips his hat at Steve.

"Antonio!" cries Steve.

"Aha, my friend," replies Antonio.
"You found me!"

At that moment, a beautiful dancer with
zigzag hair steps onto the dance floor.

Antonio swings his saxophone
high into the air and the band plays.

Steve bows and takes the dancer by the
hand. They twist and twirl across the floor.
Around and around and around they go.

Antonio blows a long silvery note
that floats through the jazz club.

Around and around spin the dancers,
twisting and turning, reeling and
whirling, into the night.

The music rises high
above the jazz club,
over the carnival city . . .

and into a new day.

Steve Goes to Carnival is a collaboration between Joshua Button and Robyn Wells.

Joshua is descended from the Walmajarri people of the Kimberley region in Western Australia. He first worked with Robyn in a literacy program in elementary school; that work resulted in the picture book *Joshua and the Two Crabs*.

In 2006, based on Joshua's love of gorillas and fascination with Brazil, they sat down at Robyn's kitchen table in Broome, Australia, and began *Steve Goes to Carnival*. It was a creative journey that lasted ten years.

The Rio de Janeiro Carnival in Brazil is the most famous carnival in the world. Every year, millions of people visit Rio to hear the music of the samba bands and see the dancers and musicians perform in parades. Some of the words in the story are in Brazilian Portuguese, the language of Brazil.

Entra, senhor	Come in, sir
favelas	shantytowns on the outskirts of the city
Feliz Carnaval	Happy Carnival
opa	a cry of surprise
sambista	a person who performs samba music or dance

FROM THE ARTISTS

Steve Goes to Carnival was born out of a long-distance love affair with the history, architecture, language, music, and food of Rio de Janeiro. Our artwork took us on an evolving journey as we pored over visual references, marveling at the textures and colors of the city: the colonial curlicues on the gateway to the zoological gardens, the yellow trams that shudder up and down the escarpments, the jumble of favelas that spill down the hillsides, and the inspired wave-patterned mosaics that line its avenues.

We used the boldness of black ink, blocks of texture, and fine lines of colored inks to create an overlapping style—a blending that celebrates Rio and the mix of peoples who bring it to life.

Thanks to Magabala Books (Australia) for their unwavering commitment to publishing this book, and to our friends and family in Broome, a community with a heartbeat of music, dance, and culture that matches the spirit of the carnival city!